This book belongs to:

_____

This book is dedicated to my Fledgling Falcons:
BJ, Colton, Fisher, James, Peter, Preston, Russell, Salina, TJ and William,
for whom this book was written. - DM

~~~

Text and Illustration ©2006 by Deirdre McLaughlin Mercier

Layout and Design: Barcita & Barcita, Inc.
Editor: Cindy Huffman

The text is set in 36-point Kev. The illustrations are mixed media collage.

English Edition:
Library of Congress Control Number: 2005938181
ISBN: 978-0-9754342-5-3

First Impression - Hardcover

Proudly manufactured in the United States of America by Worzalla, Stevens Point, WI

Bumble Bee
PUBLISHING
A Division of Bumble Bee Productions, Inc.
www.bumblebeepublishing.com
www.yesterdaywehadahurricane.com

Yesterday We Had A Hurricane

Deirdre McLaughlin Mercier

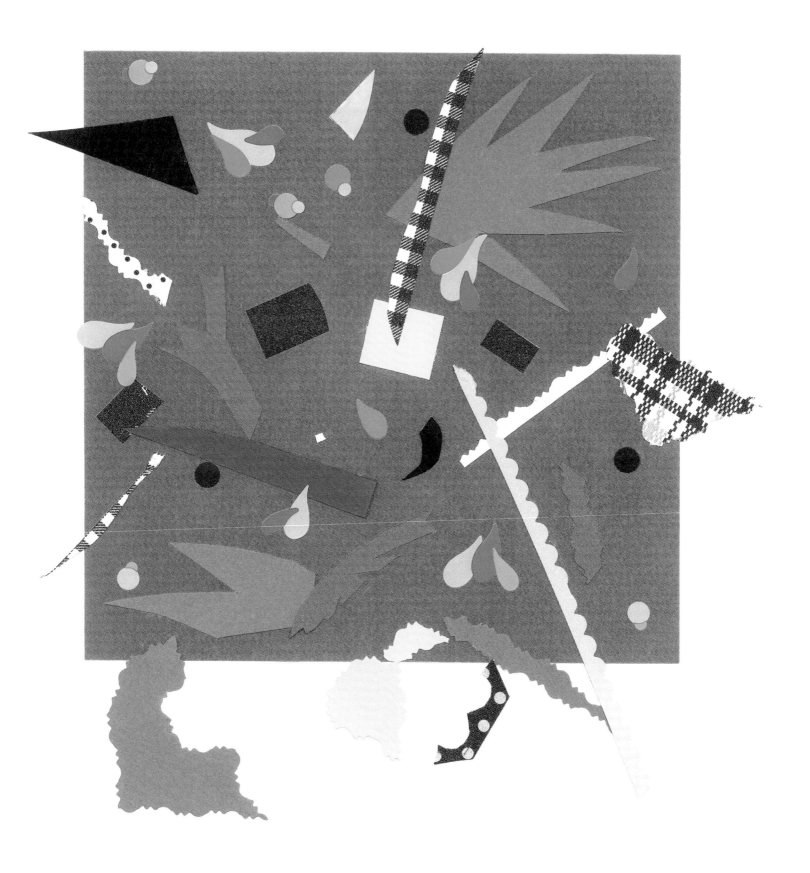

Yesterday, we had a hurricane!

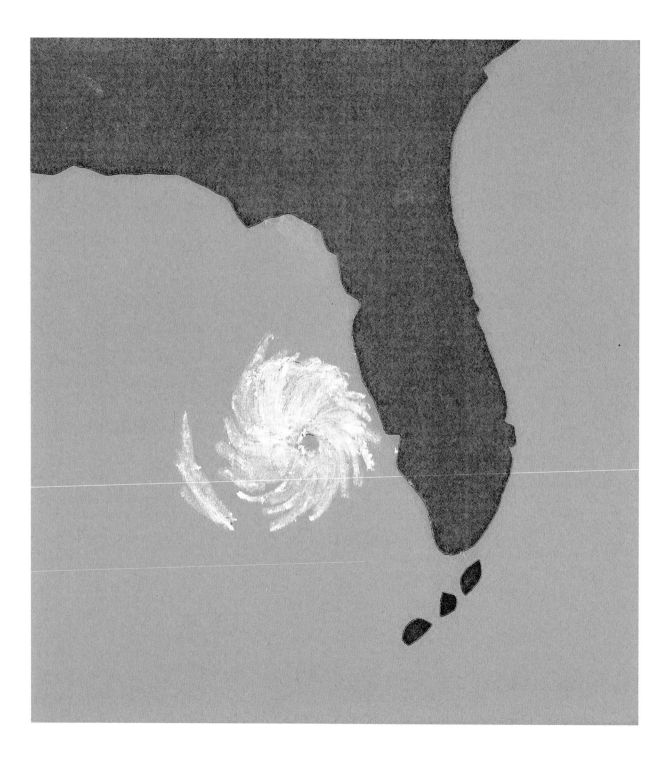

A hurricane is a big storm
that comes from the ocean.

It was very, very windy.
Tree branches fell down.

The wind was very loud.
It made a "swoosh" sound.

My dog howled at the wind.
She ran around the house.
I petted her so she would feel safe.

A tree fell on my grandmother's house.
She came to our house to be safe.

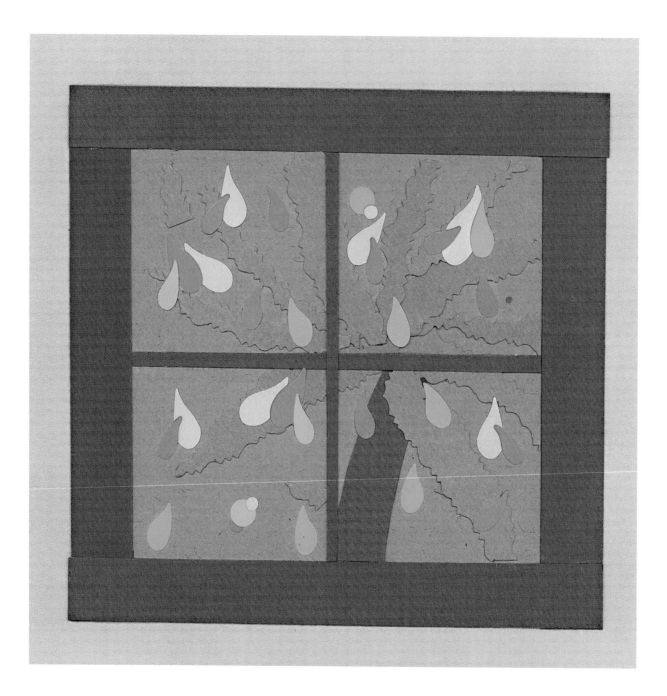

It rained very hard.
It made a "tap-tap" sound
on our windows.

Our yard got so much rain that we couldn't see the grass! There was water **everywhere!**

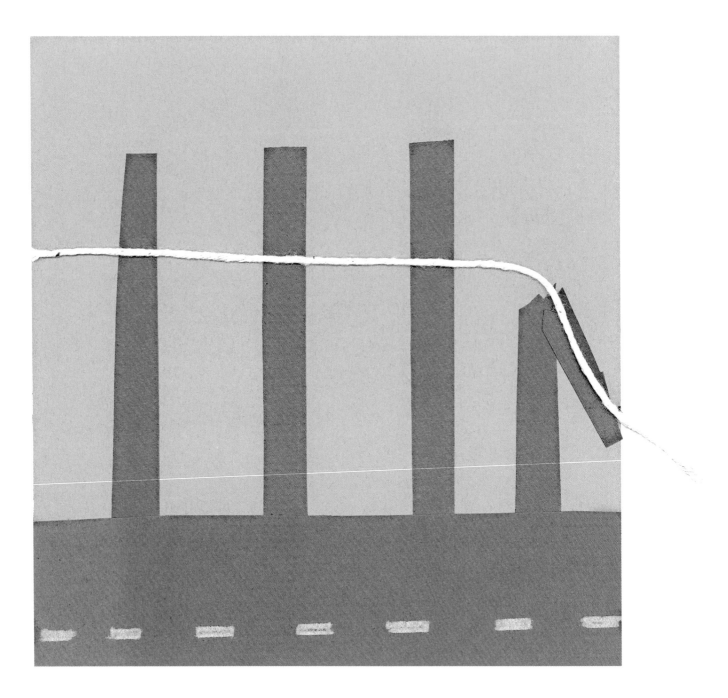

The wind blew so hard,
power lines came down.
We lost electricity.

That was scary!
But Mommy said it was okay
because we were safe.
We stayed close together.

Candles and flashlights
helped us see in the dark.
They made funny shadows.

Without power,
the stove wouldn't work.
Daddy made us peanut butter and jelly
sandwiches. They were good!

Without power, I couldn't watch TV.
I played a board game instead.

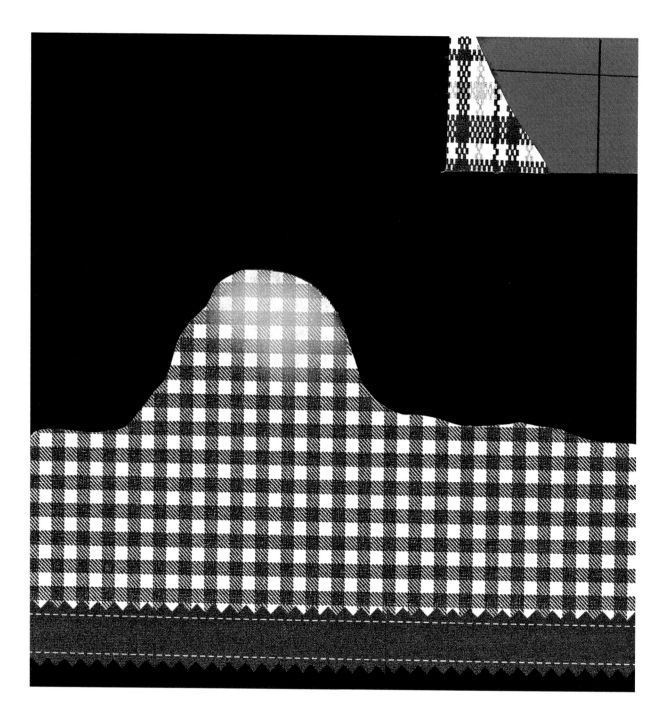

At bedtime, I played with
a flashlight under my blanket.
That was fun!

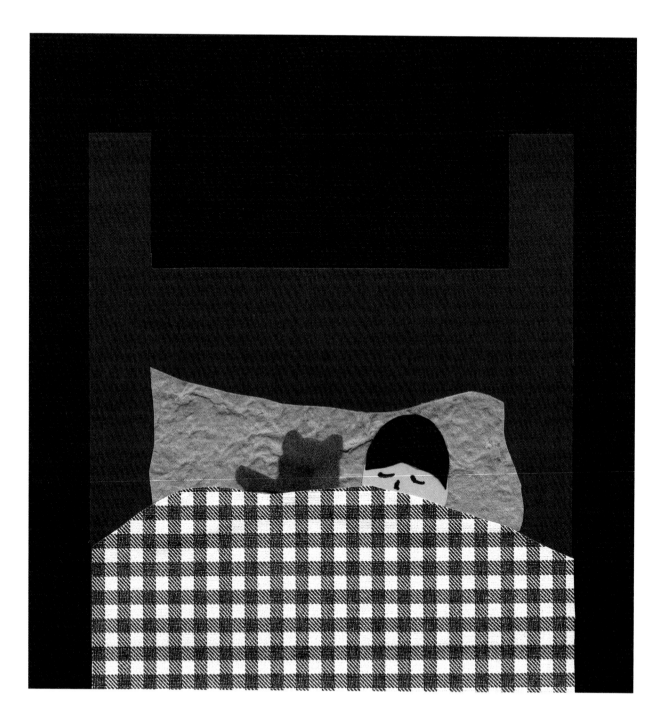

Last night I dreamed
that the hurricane went away
and left us a present.

And it did!
It left us a big mess!

ABOUT THE AUTHOR:

Deirdre Mercier has been an elementary school teacher and counselor for the past 20 years. A member of the Society of Children's Book Writers and Illustrators, she wrote *Yesterday We Had A Hurricane* for her preschool students after experiencing Hurricane Charley in 2004. She also works as a parenting educator, facilitating parenting groups on topics such as power struggles, discipline, communication, sibling rivalry, and adoption. This is her first published book. She lives with her family in Bradenton, Florida.